KICK!

THE HEIR

ISREAL KEATS

darbycreek
MINNEAPOLIS

Darby Creek
A division of Lerner Publishing Group, Inc.
241 First Avenue North
Minneapolis, MN 55401 USA

For reading levels and more information, look up this title at
www.lernerbooks.com.

The images in this book are used with the permission of: iStockphoto.com/tratong; iStockphoto.com/Purdue9394; iStockphoto.com/PhonlamaiPhoto; iStock.com/sumnersgraphicsinc.

Main body text set in Janson Text LT Std 12/17.5.
Typeface provided by Adobe Systems.

Library of Congress Cataloging-in-Publication Data

Names: Keats, Israel, author.
Title: The heir / Israel Keats.
Description: Minneapolis : Darby Creek, [2018] | Series: Kick! | Summary: Rob has always expected to be a soccer star like his father, but when his best friend and former teammate, Tyler, invites him to help form a band, Rob considers other possibilities.
Identifiers: LCCN 2017018575 (print) | LCCN 2017036379 (ebook) | ISBN 9781541500327 (eb pdf) | ISBN 9781541500211 (lb : alk. paper) | ISBN 9781541500310 (pb : alk. paper)
Subjects: | CYAC: Soccer—Fiction. | Fathers and sons—Fiction. | Friendship—Fiction. | Bands (Music)—Fiction. | High schools—Fiction. | Schools—Fiction.
Classification: LCC PZ7.1.K396 (ebook) | LCC PZ7.1.K396 Hei 2018 (print) | DDC [Fic]—dc23

LC record available at https://lccn.loc.gov/2017018575

Manufactured in the United States of America
1-43653-33470-8/29/2017

For the Lone Stars

ROB sped across the field with the soccer ball. A crowd of defenders wearing red practice jerseys formed a wall in front of him. He saw Tyler out of the corner of his eye, in position thirty feet away. Rob kicked the ball with the side of his foot. It sailed over the heads of defenders and landed in front of Tyler.

You know what to do, Ty! Rob thought. He zipped through the line of defenders and ran clear.

Tyler fired the ball back and Rob had it. He dribbled it to the goal, did a stutter step to fake out the goalie, and fired the ball right past him. The ball hit the corner of the net.

Gooooooooooaaaaaal!

Rob pumped a fist in the air and circled back to slap hands with Tyler. "Nice one!"

Mr. Gonzalez—the new economics teacher and the team's new coach—waved all the players over to the bench. This was the team's first practice with Coach Tom, as he'd asked the players to call him.

"I hope you all saw that," Coach Tom said. "It was a great example of a give-and-go."

"Tyler and I have done it a million times," Rob said.

"Since we were little kids on a Pee Wee team," Tyler added.

"What're your names?" Coach Tom looked at his clipboard.

"Tyler."

The coach checked the name on his roster. *Probably deciding the starters*, Rob thought. *Won't be a problem for Ty and me.*

"And you?" the coach asked.

"Rob," he answered.

Coach Tom checked the name with his pencil, then looked up at him. "Rob . . . Briggs? Any relation to Stephen Briggs?"

Some of the other players whispered at that. Rob ignored it. "He's my dad."

Coach Tom whistled low. "Dad is a pro soccer player," he said under his breath, pretending to jot the note down on his clipboard.

"*Former* pro," Rob said. "Now he coaches college soccer."

"Wow. I didn't even know he lived in town," the coach said.

"He's the head coach at Rodgers College."

"Glad you're playing for Fremont High, Rob. You look like your dad. Apparently you play like him too."

"Thanks."

Rob was proud of his dad—and it was cool to be the son of a professional athlete—but he was tired of being compared to him. All the other kids could be themselves, but he had to be Young Briggs, heir to soccer greatness.

He cleared his throat, desperate to change the subject, and looked over to the bench. Tyler was digging into his bag and took out his phone.

"Hey! No phones during practice!" the coach called out.

"Sorry!" Tyler said. Rob noticed that a small smile passed across his friend's face before he put his phone back in his bag.

***

"New girlfriend?" Rob asked in the locker room after practice. He was already dressed, but Tyler was sitting shirtless on the bench looking at his phone.

Rob hadn't seen his teammate since last spring. Rob had spent the first half of the summer at soccer camp and the second half with his mom in Maine.

"Nah," said Tyler, shoving the phone in his pocket and grabbing his shirt. "I mean, yeah, it's a girl. Angela Trumbull?"

Rob nodded. "I know her."

"But we're not dating," Tyler continued. "We're gonna jam." He pulled the shirt over his head.

"Jam?" Rob echoed, raising an eyebrow.

"You know. Get some people together and play music."

"But you don't play an instrument," Rob said.

"Sure I do. I took piano lessons when we were younger, remember?" Tyler stuffed his wet towel into his bag and zipped it up.

"Oh yeah, I guess." Rob zipped up his own bag. "But I thought you quit years ago."

"Well, she has this group and they need a keyboard player. So I said I'd give it a go. See how much I remember."

"Is Angela the lead singer?" Rob asked. "I saw her in a school play once. Really good."

"Yeah, she's great. I wouldn't be surprised if she signs a record deal after high school. Hopefully with me in the backup band."

Tyler glanced at the mirror across from the lockers and raked his hair with his fingers. "Hey, do you still play guitar? We could use a guitar player."

"I still play, but I've never played with other people. It's just a way to chill."

"We're getting together at my place on Saturday if you want to come. There will be pizza. And it'll be plenty chill—just hanging out and jamming."

That does sound fun, thought Rob. "Sure. I mean, maybe. If my dad lets me."

"Dude, school has barely started. There's not much homework yet."

"Yeah, but my dad has a game that evening. He wants me to go."

"It's all soccer, all the time, at the Briggs house," Tyler teased as they headed for the door.

"Yeah. Sometimes it feels that way," Rob admitted.

He expected to walk home but his dad's SUV was sitting in the parking lot. His dad wasn't in it. He was over by the equipment shed, talking to the new coach.

Uh oh, Rob thought.

"SO what do you think of the new coach?"
his dad asked as he drove them home.

"It's hard to say after one day," said Rob.
He was hot, even after the shower. It was still
August, after all. He aimed the AC at his face
to cool down.

"What did he have you do for practice?" his
dad asked.

Rob told his dad about the drills and
exercises they'd run. His dad didn't say much.

This is what I was afraid of, Rob thought.
*Dad's measuring up the new coach. Wondering if
he's good enough for "the heir."*

But his dad nodded when Rob mentioned
that the coach hollered at Tyler for checking
his phone. "That's promising. Maybe he won't

be as soft on you boys as the coach last year."

"Dad, that was JV." *Coach Stewart was a good guy. So what if he thought sportsmanship and having fun were more important than winning?*

"Mr. Gonzalez told me he's never coached before," his dad said as he rolled into the garage. "Can you believe it? They'd never do that for basketball or football."

"No, they wouldn't," Rob agreed.

He paused getting out of his seat after the SUV was parked, remembering that he'd meant to ask if he could hang out with Tyler and his friends on Saturday. *But as usual we talked about soccer the whole time.*

***

The Fremont Flyers played their first game that Thursday, against the West End Raiders. It was a "friendly" game, meaning it wouldn't count in their final record.

"Let's all play like it's for real," Coach Tom told the team in the locker room before the game. They were dressed and ready to go, but the coach wanted to talk to them before they took the field.

It's always for real when Dad is watching, Rob thought. His dad usually couldn't make Rob's games because of his own coaching, but he was there today.

"However, you can take some chances you wouldn't usually take," said the coach, "so don't play scared. See what you can do."

That sounds like something Dad would say, Rob thought. But if he played well, there was a chance his dad would let him go to Tyler's on Saturday.

That thought sent Rob charging down the field after the ball on the opening whistle. He stole the ball from a midfielder and took it to the goal. It was almost too easy as he weaved between the defenders and sped past his teammates.

The last defender came at him, trying to steal the ball. There was a fine line between "charging," which was a penalty, and "fair charging," which was allowed. Rob stayed on the "fair charging" side, using his shoulder to push the defender out of the way. The defender still came after him but was one step behind.

Rob fired off a shot. The ball bounced off the goalpost. The small crowd cheered, then groaned as the ball rolled away.

Oh well, it's not a real game anyway, he thought.

"Briggs!" Coach Tom shouted from the sideline. He waved Rob off the field and sent in a sub.

"What was that?" the coach asked when Rob jogged over to him.

"A shot on goal?" Rob said. *What did I do wrong?*

"You could have looked for a teammate to pass it to," Coach Tom said. "You don't have to win the game all by yourself."

"I know. Sorry." The joy of that opening shot drained away.

"You also came close to drawing a penalty when you strong-armed that defender."

"He did the same to me," Rob said.

"Still. He might retaliate, try to get in a cheap shot. It looked kind of rough for a game called 'a friendly.'"

Sure enough, the Raider defender kept

glaring at Rob through the rest of the game and even drew a yellow card for taunting. Rob didn't hear what the guy said, but the ref must have.

He's taking this way too personally, Rob thought. He was used to playing hard, but some high school players weren't. They hadn't played in the same leagues he had. He knew that his aggressive playing sometimes made him seem like a jerk, but that was the type of playing he was used to. That was the type of playing he needed to do if he wanted to get to the pros.

The Flyers kept up the attack and scored two more goals. Rob scored one himself and set up another. The defender kept charging, bruising Rob's shins, bumping into him and pretending it was an accident. But he'd played in enough advanced leagues and clinics to know this wasn't just another aggressive player. This guy was just trying to get back at him.

The Raiders scored one goal in the first half and another just before the end of regulation time. Now the score was three to two, and there was still a minute or two of stoppage time.

We need to tack on another goal, thought Rob, *in case the Raiders get lucky and score again.*

He moved on the ball after the drop and took it into the Raiders' side of the field. Tyler was in position for the give-and-go. It was exactly like they'd done it in practice. Rob sailed the ball over to Tyler and slipped past the defenders. Nobody was left between Rob and the net but the goaltender. *Come on, Tyler, do your thing.*

But this time the ball didn't come back to him. Rob glanced back. Tyler still had the ball and was looking wildly around the field.

What just happened? Rob wondered. *Wasn't he paying attention?*

Tyler finally tried to make the pass, but it was too late. A defender intercepted the ball and booted it to a Raiders midfielder, who passed it to a striker.

Rob hurried back to the centerline, checking to make sure he didn't pass the midfielders. His job was offense, and all he could do now was watch and wait.

The Raiders strikers advanced the ball quickly and had a shot on goal.

Nooooo! Rob couldn't do anything.

Their striker took his shot, sending the ball skidding along the ground toward the right side of the goal. The Flyers goalie threw his body sideways, got a hand on the ball, and deflected it. The ball rolled away. The Raiders could have had another shot but weren't able to get to the ball.

One of the Flyers defenders swooped in and booted the ball toward a midfielder.

Whew. That was close. If this was a real game . . . Rob ran ahead, staying slightly forward of the ball, ready to take a pass. *Well, I know what Dad would say.* He glanced up and saw his dad in the front of the bleachers, frowning.

Who am I kidding? He'll say it anyway.

***

"Pretty amateurish effort out there," his dad said as soon as Rob got into the SUV.

"Well, we *are* amateurs. We're high school kids, remember?"

"Don't be snarky. You know what I mean."

Rob looked down. "Yeah."

They had gotten more than halfway home without another word between them. "Sorry if I smell," Rob said, just to break the silence. He hadn't showered. His dad had been in a hurry to leave, so Rob had shoved his street clothes into his gym bag.

His dad didn't answer.

"I guess you're used to it, with all those sweaty college guys," Rob added. Still no answer.

He's mad at me for how Tyler played, he thought. *That makes no sense.*

"Look, Tyler's just distracted right now," Rob said. "He'll be fine. He's always been a good teammate."

"Slacking off is never acceptable," his dad grumbled.

"Dad, we won the game," Rob reminded him.

"It's not about the game, Rob. I want to know that you're growing as a player instead of learning bad habits. Like slacking off when you get a lead."

"Dad, I *am* growing as a player. I'm still playing, and working out on the weekends, and going on those long runs with you, and eating healthy, mostly . . ."

His dad sighed. "I wish you'd signed up for the club league. They have higher expectations and more experienced coaches."

"I like playing with Tyler and the guys," Rob told him. *We've had this discussion a thousand times.* "The club league will still be there in the spring."

"Tyler is a good kid, but he's not a serious athlete," said his dad. "And he's the second-best player on the team! You might find you can't keep up anymore. You know what happens to astronauts who live up in space for a while?"

"Yes, I know." Aside from soccer, his dad's favorite topic was science. "They live in low gravity for a while and have trouble walking and doing normal stuff when they come back to Earth."

"I don't want that to happen to you."

"I'm not moving to space, Dad. I'm playing high school soccer."

"You get my point."

"Well, yeah," Rob admitted. *How many athletes get a lecture from their dad because one of their teammates didn't play well?* he wondered.

Another thought crossed his mind.

How can I ask to skip the college game to hang out with the slacker Dad is mad about?

***

So Rob didn't ask. He went to the game on Saturday.

The students at Rodgers College packed the stands, turning the stadium into a sea of teal and orange. They chanted and sang and waved noisemakers.

OK, this is fun, Rob thought as the team took the field and the stands exploded.

The game itself was sloppy. The Rodgers players were skilled players, but they were out of sync. They missed easy passes and got confused about who was guarding what player.

As the coach's kid, Rob was allowed to sit

on the sidelines with the players. But his dad was too busy to talk to him. He watched as his dad encouraged one player after a missed goal and scolded another one for misfiring a pass.

The players all had different accents. One player was from Ghana, one from Germany, one from Colombia. Rob heard the word "Coach" said a dozen different ways. *They come from all over the world to learn soccer from Dad*, he thought. He felt a surge of pride in his father.

"Great guys, huh?" his dad said when he finally had a chance to talk to him. He stood next to where Rob was seated, staring out at the field with his hands on his hips.

"Yeah," said Rob.

"I know they aren't playing that well. They all have their own style of soccer and have to get on the same page." His dad paused to survey the team once again and then grinned. "But in a few weeks we'll be in sync and then I think we'll play some great soccer."

He really likes his players, Rob thought. *Even when they aren't playing that well.*

"I guess it's not much fun to watch now, huh?" his dad asked.

"It's always fun to watch," Rob said. Even though he truly didn't mind watching the game, Rob had other activities on his mind— specifically, hanging out with Tyler and his friends. His dad was clearly in a good mood. Rob figured it would be a good time to take a chance.

"But hey, can I go hang out with Tyler? He lives nearby. I could walk."

"Yeah, I know where he lives," his dad said. "I'll come get you after the game."

"Awesome." *I can't believe he's letting me go,* he thought.

"Have fun," his dad said. Rob's face must have shown his surprise because his dad smiled and waved him off, saying, "I'm too busy here to talk to you much anyway. And you won't learn anything, except what a good team looks like before they knock the rust off."

"Thanks, Dad!" Rob took off before his dad could change his mind.

Just after he left the stadium, Rob heard a

roar of cheering and felt a brief twang of regret.

I must have missed something good, he thought. *But I'm free for a few hours. Free from talking about soccer. Free from being the star of a team or the coach's son. I can be a normal high school kid, hanging out with friends on a Saturday night.*

"WHERE'S your ax?" Tyler asked when he swung open the door.

"My what?"

"Your ax. Your guitar."

"Oh, yeah. I forgot." Rob felt foolish. *I was looking forward to hanging out with friends. I forgot this was a jam session.* "It was kind of last minute, all right?"

Tyler smiled. "No worries. Come on in."

Rob looked around the house as he walked inside. It seemed like no one else was home. "Where's your mom and sisters?"

"They went to a movie so we could play."

Tyler led him downstairs to the cramped basement. There was a girl with bleached hair and a nose ring sitting by the water heater.

"Angela, right?" Rob asked. "I think we have a couple of classes together."

"You're Rob," she said with a nod.

"And this is Liz," said Tyler, pointing out a slightly older girl with dyed black hair. She was sitting behind a drum kit squeezed in between a metal shelf and the washing machine.

"Hey," she said. "I know you. You're a big soccer star."

Rob shrugged. "There's no such thing as a big soccer star at Fremont. Not like being a basketball player."

"False modesty," said Liz. "I like it."

"He also plays air guitar like a champ," Tyler said. The girls laughed.

"I guess I'll have to tonight," Rob admitted. "I forgot my guitar."

"Are you right-handed?" asked the drummer. "My brother's guitar is in my van."

"Really?" He looked at her in surprise. "That would be awesome. And, yeah, I am."

"Well, we're in business." She jumped up and left, returning a minute later with a guitar case and an amplifier. "Let's rock."

The guitar was electric and Rob was used to acoustic. The strings were easier to hold down but the slightest touch made a lot of noise.

Liz tapped her sticks to set the time and Tyler tapped out a bass rhythm on his keyboard. *Not bad for a guy who quit playing years ago*, thought Rob.

Rob played a song he knew, one he figured everyone else would know too.

"Play it in G," Angela said. Tyler smoothly switched keys. Rob switched too, but not as smoothly. Angela started to sing.

Tyler was right about her. She was amazing.

Rob liked the crunchy sound of the electric guitar. As he got used to it, he started to work in fills and flourishes, ones he'd learned from a book and used at home.

"Hey!" Liz shouted over the drums. "You're good!"

"Told you," Tyler said to her.

You did? thought Rob. *I can't even remember the last time you've heard me play. Maybe at soccer camp two years ago?*

Angela had printed off sheet music for a few classic rock songs, and they muddled their way through them. Rob couldn't read music, but the chords were shown along with the notes. He played along as best he could, improvising when he had to. They sounded all right as a group, especially when Angela was singing.

She's like the striker on a soccer team, Rob thought. *We set her up and let her score.* Then he scolded himself. *Stop thinking about soccer.*

Finally, they took a break, moving upstairs to the living room. It was messy compared to Rob's. There was a pile of mail on the coffee table, books and forgotten cups on an end table.

People actually live in here, he thought. He mostly hung out in his room and his dad was never home, so their living room was rarely actually used.

The girls sat on the couch. "I'll go put some frozen pizza in the oven," said Tyler. He went off to the kitchen.

Rob plopped down in an armchair. His left hand felt stiff. He opened and closed his hand to loosen it up.

"That was fun," he said.

"You're good," Angela told him. "But it sounds like you're not used to playing in a band?"

"Nope, this is my first time."

"In that case, wow. Really good for the first time playing with others."

"Thanks. What about you? Have you jammed a lot?"

"Oh, yeah. Liz and I were in a band that just broke up," Angela told him.

"Ah."

"That's why we're starting a new one."

"Awesome," said Rob. "Good luck finding the other members."

She raised an eyebrow.

"What?" *Did it come out sarcastic?* he wondered. "Seriously, you and Liz are good. I don't think you'll have any trouble."

"This *is* our new group," she said. "Me and Liz and Tyler, and a guitar player when we find one. Ty thought maybe it could be you?"

"Really? I thought we were just messing

around. Tyler?" Rob looked for his friend, but Tyler was still in the kitchen.

Rob cleared his throat, suddenly nervous. "Well, Tyler and I can't be in a band. Not a serious one, not now. We've got soccer. He probably told you that."

Liz sat up on the couch. Angela narrowed her eyes. "No," she said. "He didn't tell us that." The girls exchanged a glance.

"Oh." *Man, I just messed up*, he thought.

He kept his mouth shut until Tyler got back with the pizza. The four of them ate and talked about school, their favorite bands, and whatever else came to mind. Not soccer, which meant Rob didn't have as much to say.

After dinner, Angela and Liz headed back downstairs. Rob and Tyler followed.

They were surprised to see Liz packing her drum kit.

"Don't you want to play some more?" Tyler asked.

"Not tonight. It's getting late," she said.

Rob and Tyler helped them carry pieces of equipment to Liz's van, then went back down for the rest of it. Tyler tried to grab a stand, but Liz took it from him. "We got it from here, thanks."

"Almost forgot your brother's guitar," Angela said, grabbing the case and amp. "Later." She and Liz headed upstairs.

Rob and Tyler were left alone, Tyler still tapping out bass lines on the keyboard. "They kind of left in a hurry," he said sadly. "I wonder why?"

"I might have ruined everything," Rob admitted.

"Huh?" Tyler stopped playing and looked at him.

"I told them you weren't serious about this band," said Rob. "I mean, I didn't know they didn't know. Sorry, man."

"Hm," Tyler grunted.

"But really, if they think this is going to turn into a real band, you have to tell them. You can't commit to something like that until after soccer season."

"Rob. Dude." Tyler gave him a hard look.

"Yeah?"

"I *am* serious about the band. I've been waiting to see if they want me to join. But if they do invite me, I'm going to do it."

Rob frowned. "But what about—"

Tyler continued over him. "And I'll quit soccer."

***

Rob's father pulled into the driveway a few minutes later.

"Tough loss in overtime," he said as soon as Rob climbed into the passenger seat. That answered Rob's question before he asked it. "But what about you? Did you have fun?" He pulled out of the driveway and started for home.

"Sure. But Tyler might quit the team." Rob was still reeling from the news.

"That's too bad." His dad gave him a sideways look before turning his eyes back to the road. *He thinks it's best if Tyler quits the team*, Rob figured. *Because he thinks Tyler is a slacker*.

"We've been playing soccer together since we were six," Rob reminded him.

"You can still be friends, right?"

"Yeah, but it'll be weird not having him as a teammate."

"Mhmm."

I have to put this in soccer terms so you can understand, thought Rob.

"He's always there when I need to make a pass. And he always sends the ball back to me exactly when I expect it." *Except in our last game*, he remembered. "Usually, I mean."

Suddenly he wanted to talk to his mother. They talked every Sunday, so he'd have the chance to tell her about all this tomorrow. She would understand. She was more willing to talk to him about life outside of soccer.

His dad turned to look at him at the next red light.

"I know it's hard," he said. "I've said goodbye to a lot of teammates in my life. It gets worse as you move on to college and then the pros. Guys are always getting cut or getting hurt. You're still chasing your dream and they're trying to figure out what else they can do with their lives."

"Yeah." *So maybe Tyler's smart for figuring out what else he can do now. Maybe I should do that too.* A thought slowly crossed his mind. *I'm not mad at Tyler. I'm jealous.*

ON Monday morning a curly-haired kid from Rob's history class held up a hand as he walked into the room.

"Good game, Briggs," the boy said.

"Yeah, nice goal!" said another.

Rob grinned and thanked them as he walked past them. This was one of the best parts about playing for the school instead of a club league. After a win, at least a handful of other students congratulated him. Even after a loss, some would say "tough game," or "nice try." When he was on a club team, no one even knew that he'd played.

He noticed Angela sitting in the back. She was in a small group of girls who wore skinny jeans and concert T-shirts, some with dyed hair or lip piercings. None of them said anything to him about the game—they barely even looked at him. He nodded at Angela as he found his own desk. She barely nodded back, but he didn't take it personally. Students stuck to their cliques at Fremont.

The teacher rambled through the early part of the Industrial Revolution. Rob tried to keep up, scribbling notes. As they left after class, Angela gave him a friendly nudge on the arm.

"Hey," she said as she passed. He barely had a chance to say hello back before she disappeared into the crowd in the hallway.

Maybe she doesn't want to be seen talking to a jock, Rob thought. As he paused, a group of students swooped in to pat him on the back and talk about the game. *Or maybe she thinks I don't want to be seen talking to her?*

***

The Flyers had their first official game on Thursday. It was an away game, and Tyler wasn't on the team bus. Rob would have asked Coach Tom about it, but he was talking with someone on his cell.

Tyler wasn't waiting at the Central High School soccer field, either.

Rob sent a text: *WHERE ARE YOU??* But he had to put away his phone before he could get an answer.

"We're down a starting striker," Coach Tom said. "Elliot, you'll move up to striker with Ben and Luis. Malcolm, you move into Elliot's midfield slot. Grayson, you'll play defense today."

"What happened to Tyler?" Ben asked.

"Your guess is as good as mine," Coach Tom said.

Ugh, Rob thought. *Tyler is going to get kicked off the team before he even has a chance to quit.*

The Central High Cougars were bigger than most soccer players. The back four could have been football players. They hung back on their side of the field and made a series of passes, keeping the ball safe but not trying to score. The Flyers offensive players ran themselves ragged trying to get to the ball. The Cougars always booted it away before they got there.

That's their trap, and we're falling right into it, Rob realized. *Once we're tuckered out they'll go on attack. We need to put more pressure on them.*

He studied the pattern of their passes and guessed correctly where the next pass would go. He streaked into the passing lane and intercepted the ball.

One of the Cougars took a step toward him but stopped. Rob dribbled the ball forward. The player backed up. Two other defenders moved in. Rob had nowhere to go.

This is where I would pass it to Tyler, he thought.

He looked around and saw Ben. Rob booted the ball his way, broke free of the defender, and found an open zone. Ben fired the ball back toward him but aimed badly. The ball rolled behind Rob. He whirled around and tried to recover it, but now the Cougars had it again.

"Lousy pass," Rob grumbled.

The Cougars continued to pass the ball back and forth across the field without a scoring drive. When they at last moved the ball into Flyers territory, Elliot was caught by surprise. He ran after their striker but the Cougar had a shot. Deondre, Fremont's goalie, dived, but it was too late—the ball got by him and rolled into the net.

The whistle sounded for the goal. The Cougars traded high fives.

"They got lucky," Luis grumbled as the Flyers regrouped for the kickoff.

"It's not luck. They have a plan, and it's working," Rob said.

The Cougars kept up the same strategy: now that they'd scored one goal, they basically hogged the ball, rarely taking a chance on actually scoring. Rob knew the Cougars were trying to keep the ball away from him and his teammates for as long as they could. The clock ticked away. The Flyers were tired and frustrated.

Near the end of the first half, Rob took away a pass. This time, he didn't bother looking for a teammate. He took the ball as far as he could and fired a shot from thirty yards back.

The ball veered to the left of the goal. The whistle sounded for halftime.

Rob shuffled to the bench, drenched in sweat and exhausted.

"I had to take the shot," he told Coach Tom. "Time was running out."

"I know," the coach said. "Good try."

The team gathered around the bench, some of the players dumping water from their water bottles on their heads to cool off. Nobody looked happy.

"I've never seen a team keep the ball like that," the coach said.

"What do we do?" another player asked.

"Press them hard in the second half," the coach instructed. "You midfielders move up and support the offense. We'll leave just the back four to defend."

"That could be risky if they get past us," Deondre said, rubbing the back of his head with a towel. "We'll be outnumbered."

"We have to take a chance," Coach said.

"What do you want us to do when we get

the ball?" Elliot asked.

"Give the ball to Rob."

Rob looked up in surprise. Coach was serious.

"And if you're passing to him, don't miss," Coach said.

He didn't say if he was referring to anyone specifically, but Rob noticed the way Ben hung his head. Rob was all too familiar with the pressure Ben must be feeling.

Still, making a decent pass was, like, basic soccer. Rob took a long drink of water and toweled off. He was antsy to begin the next half.

After the kickoff, the Flyers sent seven guys into Cougars territory, driving the ball toward the net. Ben sent the ball skipping toward Rob. It was a bad pass, but Rob raced toward it and kicked for the goal. The ball shot through the goalie's hands and into the net. The game was tied at 1–1.

The Cougars kept up their ball-hogging strategy. They didn't even try to score again. It seemed like they were content to tie.

Late in the game Elliot passed Rob the

ball. But defenders were crowded around him. Rob passed it on to Ben, who was in a better position to score. Ben passed it back to him.

Come on, Rob thought. *Do I really have to do this by myself?*

He faked a pass, took the ball around the defenders, and took a shot. The ball zoomed past two defenders and the goalie and rolled into the net.

Rob's teammates and the Flyers fans cheered, while the Cougars fans quieted down, stunned. Their team had dominated all afternoon, but the Flyers were ahead with only a few minutes left to play.

At last the Cougars had to be aggressive on offense. It left their backfield open, and when the Flyers got the ball they were able to quickly zoom downfield. Once again Rob had to take the shot, and this time it was an easy one.

"Hat trick!" Ben shouted, offering a high five as they trotted off the field. Rob slapped his hand but he didn't feel that good about it.

"You should have taken that second goal

yourself," he said.

"Coach said to give you the ball," Ben said. "He was right. You're the best player on the team by far. That goal was amazing."

***

After the game, Rob showered, dressed, and climbed back onto the bus without talking to anyone. He sat in the front by himself, wanting to be alone. He wished he knew what was happening with Tyler.

His phone buzzed and he pulled it out of his pocket, hoping for a reply from Tyler, but it was a text from his dad.

How was the game? Did you win?

Good. 3–1 us, he replied. He didn't feel like mentioning that he'd scored all three goals.

Coach Tom climbed on and sat down next to Rob.

"You all right?" he asked. "You look pretty glum for a guy who won the game single-handedly. I guess I should say *single-footedly*." He chuckled.

"What happened to me not needing to win

the game all by myself?" Rob asked.

"Huh?"

"You said that last game. But today you told everyone to give me the ball. So they did, every single time."

"I didn't have time to explain a complex strategy," Coach Tom said. "'Give Rob the ball' was simple. And it worked."

"Hm," Rob grunted. He slumped lower in his seat, looking out the window. "I don't want to win games single-footedly."

"Hey, I was kidding. That was a team effort. The other guys worked hard to get you the ball." He jerked his head to the back of the bus. "Why are you giving them the silent treatment?"

"I didn't mean to," Rob said.

"Like it or not, you're a team leader," the coach said. "Go talk to them."

"Yeah, sure." Rob stood up, taking a deep breath. He forced his mouth into a smile and headed down the bus aisle to talk to his teammates.

HIS dad wasn't home, which was normal during the college soccer season. Rob's mom had been working in state parks since before Rob was born, so she was always living in the middle of nowhere. For the past few years, that middle of nowhere had been somewhere in Maine. The town she lived in didn't have much soccer. The high school didn't have a team, and joining a traveling team would mean long drives. So, even though Rob's dad was gone a lot, his house was the better option for Rob during the school year.

That also meant Rob was alone a lot, but he didn't mind.

He was grilling a couple of ham and cheese sandwiches when his phone buzzed. It was a text from Tyler.

Sorry I missed the game, his message said. *I tried to call Coach but couldn't get ahold of him.*

That made sense, since Coach had been talking on his phone during the entire bus ride.

Rob stuffed the phone in his pocket and moved the sandwiches to a plate. He piled on some cut vegetables and carried his dinner to the dining room.

What happened to you? he tapped out with one hand, eating with the other.

The band thing is on, Tyler wrote.

Congrats, he typed. *Got a name yet?*

Tyler's next message came at the moment Rob sent his.

Soccer thing is off.

Rob had known it might happen, but the news still hit him like a hard-kicked soccer ball to the gut. But he knew there was no use in trying to talk Tyler out of this.

Dumb name, he texted back, adding a winking emoji.

After scarfing down his dinner, Rob went up to his room and strummed a few songs on his guitar. He thought about how good it felt to play with Tyler and his friends. He found himself imagining what a song would sound like if Angela were singing or if Tyler were accompanying him on the keyboard.

The door creaked open and his dad peered in. "You didn't tell me you scored all three goals."

"Uh, yeah," Rob said. "I did." He set down the guitar. "How did you know?"

"Your coach told me."

"Oh? You talked to him?"

"He called me."

That's kind of weird, Rob thought. "Did he call you as my coach or as your biggest fan?"

"We'd already talked today," his dad said with a shrug. "He asked me for coaching advice on the way to your game."

"I get it." *So that's who Coach was talking to on the bus.* "What did you tell him?"

"Basic soccer stuff."

"Like what?"

"Don't let the other team set the tone. Play to your strengths. That kind of thing."

"Give the ball to your best player?" Rob asked.

"Sure. There are worse strategies."

"Dad, Coach told the other guys to pass the ball to me. They wouldn't take their own shots, even when they had a better chance. It turned into the Rob Briggs show."

"Oh," his dad said simply. He didn't seem the least bit apologetic.

"Did you tell him to do that?" he asked.

"Not in so many words. I just told him to make sure you were getting challenged."

"Aha! I knew it."

"Rob, I didn't know how he'd apply my advice. But I *do* know you guys were losing before he made that change. And then you won the game."

"I guess," Rob admitted.

"What your coach did was good strategy," his dad said. "It's not unusual for a team to build around a scoring threat. And it's good for you as a player."

"But now there's a lot more pressure on me," Rob said.

"Pressure turns coal into diamonds," his dad said. Geology was another of his dad's favorite topics.

But what does too much pressure do to astronauts? Rob wanted to ask.

"Don't forget your homework," his dad said as he left the room.

"I won't." Rob looked at his guitar. *I wonder if Dad liked what I was playing,* he thought. *I wonder if he even noticed.*

***

Angela stopped him as he walked into history on Monday morning. They stood in the hall just outside the door.

"What did you write about for class?" she asked. They'd been assigned to pick a major invention of the Industrial Revolution and write about how it changed society.

"Roads," he said. "What about you?"

"Textiles."

"Wow, fascinating," he said jokingly.

"Actually it was," she said. *Ugh, I'm acting like the dumb jock she thinks I am,* he realized.

At that moment a hand slapped him on the shoulder.

"Hat trick! Awesome game!" It was the curly-haired kid.

"Yeah, thanks," said Rob. The kid went into the classroom and Rob turned back to Angela. "Uh, so, how was your weekend? Did you practice with Tyler and Liz?"

"Yeah. We tried out a guitar player but he was pretty terrible," she said. "And a jerk."

"Too bad," Rob said. He was kind of relieved to hear it.

"What about you?" Angela asked.

"I went on a five-mile run with my dad and did some drills in the yard. Then I just chilled at home the rest of the weekend. Did homework. Called my mom."

"Are you a runner too?"

"No, we run to stay in shape for soccer," he said. "I mean, I do. My dad runs with me to stay healthy." *And to make sure I don't start slacking*, he thought.

"You sure are into soccer," she said.

"Well, you know my dad," he explained.

Angela just blinked at him and he realized that, actually, she probably didn't. "I mean, yeah, I am, but I do have other interests."

"Like guitar," she said.

"And roads," he added. She laughed.

"You should play with us again," she said. "We sound good together."

"Yeah," he said. "I totally should."

***

"We're going to look at scoring attacks," Coach said at practice after school. It was raining hard, so he'd taken the team into his economics classroom to talk about strategy. "What's the main strategy for the offense on a scoring attack? Ben?"

"To score a goal?"

"Well, yes. But how do you do that? Rob?"

Rob looked up from where he'd been staring into space. "Keep the ball until the other team messes up?"

"Exactly," Coach replied. "You need to recognize a mistake and take advantage." He gave examples of defensive mistakes that could be turned into goals. He drew on the whiteboard and showed videos on the projector. A lot of the videos were sports bloopers and kept the team laughing.

"I'm going to show a video from about twenty years ago," Coach said just before practice ended. He gave Rob a look.

Uh oh, Rob thought. *Hope it's not the one I think it is.*

Coach tapped on his laptop keyboard and a video projected onto the whiteboard. Rob recognized it immediately. The game was between the US and Uruguay. *Did you have to pick that one?* Rob thought.

There was his father looking really young. The camera followed him as he zipped around the field, passing the ball back and forth with two other players. Uruguay's defenders kept up, finding their way into any gap between the man with the ball and the net. The US kept charging at full throttle and refused to give up the ball. And then the big moment came. Two of Uruguay's defenders paused for a split second.

"You got this?" one seemed to ask.

"No, I think it's you," the other seemed to say.

But it was too late. Stephen Briggs saw the gap in coverage and rocketed the ball between them. The goalie watched the ball blur by.

Coach froze the video. "That goal tied the game," he said.

The US lost in penalty time, Rob knew. *But that goal was pretty great.*

"There are three things the US team does here," said Coach. "Remember it as three S's." He held up a finger as he said each one. "*Sustain* the attack. *See* a mistake. *Seize* the opportunity."

"What about number four, *score* a goal?" Elliot said. The team laughed.

"Fine. Four S's," the coach said. "Let's watch the video again and study the ways the US team sustains the attack until they see a mistake." He hit the replay button. "And see how Rob's dad—sorry, Rob . . . see how Stephen Briggs seizes the opportunity."

***

Band have a name yet? Rob texted to Tyler the next day.

Since Tyler had quit the team, they barely saw each other anymore. They didn't even have lunch at the same time. Rob knew the band members were still looking for a guitar player.

Maybe Ice Bomb, Tyler texted back. *Good name? Be honest.*

Meh, Rob answered.

OK. No name then. No guitarist either. What's up with you?

Soccer. School. What else?

Want to jam Saturday?

Sure. His dad had a game, but it was on the road. He would be gone all day and home late.

Bring a guitar this time! Tyler reminded him. *Liz's brother took his back.*

Right. Will do.

He was going to need an electric guitar. The acoustic guitar was fine for playing alone, but Rob figured he'd need an electric guitar if he was going to play with a rock band. Money wasn't a problem. Rob had saved a lot of his allowance.

He worked out a plan: He could get off the

school bus early on Friday. There was a stop near a strip mall that had a music shop. Rob could walk home from there.

He wished he could do it sooner, but first there was another away game.

"I'VE never heard of the Winfield Rush," Ben said on the bus. "We've never played them before."

Rob listened but was distracted. He couldn't stop thinking about what kind of guitar he wanted to buy.

"Winfield is a new science magnet school," Coach Tom explained. "They don't have a football team, so soccer is their big fall sport."

Rob tried to put guitar thoughts out of his mind and focus on their next opponent. A school that specialized in science didn't seem like a huge threat.

"A bunch of nerds, huh?" Elliot smirked.

"They might surprise you," said Coach.

Science and soccer, Rob thought. *Dad would love it here.*

They reached the school. The building had a large dome on the roof.

"Planetarium?" Ben guessed.

"That's kind of cool," said Rob as the bus rolled by and parked by the soccer field.

The bleachers were packed like Fremont's stands were only on football Fridays. The fans stood and cheered when the Rush ran out.

The game started. The Rush zipped around the field and made a lot of short passes. They did catch the Flyers by surprise, but they couldn't turn the attack into a score.

Once again Ben and Elliot kept passing to Rob. He fired and missed. Fired and missed again. *What's wrong with me?*

Late in the half, one of the Rush players dribbled the ball into scoring position. He stopped the ball with his toe and took a step back.

What is he doing? Rob wondered. *Does he think this is a free kick?*

Someone should have simply kicked the ball away, but the closest defender froze. The Rush player stepped forward and kicked the ball as hard as he could. It sailed smoothly toward the goal. Deondre dived for it but the ball hooked left, bounced off the goal frame, and went into the net. The Rush crowd cheered wildly.

Rob shook his head, still not sure how this had just happened, when the buzzer signaling the end of the half went off. It was a welcome break—the Flyers were losing, one to nothing.

"What happened there?" Coach Tom asked Alex, the defender who'd given up the goal.

"I didn't know what was going on," Alex said. "It took a weird turn."

"Everything about this game is weird," said Ben. "Rob keeps blowing it."

"Sorry," said Rob. "I don't know why."

"You're not blowing it on purpose, are you?" Coach asked. "Trying to make some kind of point?"

"No," said Rob, shocked. "I swear. But if you guys get a clean shot, take it." He looked at Ben and Elliot.

Coach gave him a long look. *I don't think you believe me,* Rob thought. *But I'm just having an off day.*

The Flyers finally scored a goal when Rob did a give-and-go with Ben. This time Rob set up the shot. Ben surprised the goalie by kicking straight for the goal instead of passing it to Rob again.

The rest of the game was scoreless, so they went into a penalty shoot-out. Each team had three shots at goal, and they had to use three different players. Coach put Elliot, Ben, and Rob down to kick.

The Rush kicked first. The same player who had scored their only goal kicked the ball hard and sent it spinning toward the net. Deondre missed it.

He's got some kind of tricky way of kicking it, like throwing a curveball, Rob realized. *That's why he backed up last time. I wonder if he's applying some kind of scientific principle.*

Elliot missed his shot. The second Rush player also missed. Ben's ball sailed just past the Rush goalie's fingertips, tying up the game. The third Rush player tried the kicking trick but judged it wrong and barely grazed the top of the ball with his heel. The ball rolled about three feet and died on the grass. The Winfield fans cheered for him anyway.

Either they are the best sports fans ever or they really don't understand soccer, Rob thought.

Now it was up to him to win the game.

Rob cleared his head. He didn't think about his dad, or Tyler, or school, or the band. He just saw the ball, the goalie, and the net. He charged at the ball and kicked it squarely, right for the near corner of the net. The goalie dived but missed.

The Flyers had won by one point. The Winfield fans cheered.

They have to know they just saw a victory slip away, Rob thought. *They really are just good sports. I almost wish I went here.*

***

The next day Rob bought an electric guitar and amplifier at the music store. Once the used Fender was in his hands, he had to have it. He loved the way it felt and the way it sounded. He also loved the look, with a red flame burst radiating from the neck. It was cheap, and Rob was worried somebody would buy it before he came back to get it.

Now he was lugging the guitar case and amplifier home, along with his backpack. It was about a mile, which was fine for a walk but a long way to carry so much stuff. It was a good thing he was already in decent shape.

He reached his house and looked up. His dad's SUV was in the driveway.

It's not in the garage, which means he's leaving again, Rob thought.

He thought about taking another lap around the neighborhood to avoid his dad, but he figured his dad would see the guitar eventually anyway. *Might as well get this over with.*

Rob marched up the walk, feeling as nervous as he did before a big game. He set the guitar case and amp in the hall. His dad stepped out of the kitchen, wearing a jacket and tie.

"What's that?" he asked, looking at the equipment as if Rob had brought home a pet boa constrictor.

"An electric guitar and amp," Rob said. "I used my own money," he quickly added.

"Hm."

"I might join a band," he added. Might as well get it all out there. "I can play on the days I don't have soccer." His dad still didn't say anything. "Is that OK?"

"You have workouts the days you don't have practice," his dad said. "I don't want you to spread yourself too thin."

"I won't," Rob promised. "Dad, I really want to do this."

I shouldn't have asked for permission, he realized. *Now he can say no.*

But his dad didn't say no. He did stare at the guitar in confusion. "Where does all this interest in guitar suddenly come from, anyway?" he asked.

"I've been playing for years," Rob reminded him.

"Yeah, but you were never serious about it."

"I never had a chance to be serious about anything besides soccer," Rob said.

"I get it," his dad said. "We have kept you pretty busy. But now's not the best time. You're at a critical time in your career."

Huh? Rob thought. *I have a career already? I thought I was still just prepping for one.*

"Now is when the guys who play soccer as a hobby drop out and the guys who are serious and talented—guys like you—move on. Now is when you need to focus more than ever, Rob."

The words *career* and *focus* made Rob feel panicky. *It's too much pressure*, he thought. *Diamond or no diamond.*

"Dad, maybe I'm one of those guys who does play as a hobby. Did you ever think about that?"

"You're the one who begged to go to soccer camp just a few months ago," his dad said. "Even though it meant missing half your summer with your mother."

"I know. Soccer used to be all I thought about," Rob said, "but now . . . now I'm thinking about other things. Maybe even guitar lessons."

"Rob, we've invested a lot of time and money in soccer. Skills clinics, club leagues, camps. Some of my players grew up with nothing but an old ball to kick around. They would give anything to have had the opportunities you've had."

"I know," said Rob. "I get it." *So no guitar lessons, let alone a band.* "I can take the guitar back and get a refund."

"You don't have to go that far," said his dad. "It'll still be a perfectly good guitar when you do have a chance to take lessons."

But when will that be? Rob wondered. *When I retire from the pros?*

His dad looked at the clock. "I'm late. I have to go meet some people." He hurried toward the door. "There's spaghetti in the fridge that you can heat up."

"Thanks."

"We'll talk more later," his dad said as he left. As one of the big shots on campus, he was always going to fancy dinners and events.

Rob went up to his room and plugged the guitar into the new amp. He twisted the knob all the way. That was one good thing about his dad being gone: he could crank it up. He experimented with the whammy bar, making the notes wail and scream.

He glanced up at the posters of soccer players and pennants from his favorite teams. The whole wall was covered. He took a couple of posters down. *I need to make room for something else*, he thought. *Maybe I don't have time for guitar, but Dad can't complain about wall space.*

"WHOA," Tyler said when Rob carried in the guitar on Saturday. "You went all out."

"Not really," Rob said. "It was used."

"Come on in. The girls are already set up." Tyler led Rob to the basement. Liz had set her drum kit in the usual place next to the washing machine. Angela was perched on a stool next to the hot water heater.

"Hey," Angela said.

"New guitar?" Liz asked.

"New to me. I can't play rock and roll on an acoustic," Rob said, trying to shrug it off. But he did beam with pride when he unpacked the guitar and pulled the strap over his neck.

"It looks good on you," Angela said.

Rob answered by striking the strings and working the whammy bar. The others laughed.

The four of them played for an hour, playing through all the songs from last time and a couple of new ones. Rob found it easier this time. He was now used to following Liz's rhythm. He even tried a solo, and when he was done the other three cheered for him.

Later, they sat in the living room again and munched on snacks. "This was awesome," Liz said. "We sound like a real band."

"Yeah," Tyler said. "That solo was really great, Rob."

Rob couldn't help but smile at that. He wasn't used to getting compliments in anything but soccer. *Maybe I am good at this.*

***

"Today will be a challenge," Coach Tom said before the next game. It was at home, against the Harrison High Bulls.

Ben groaned. "Last time we played 'em, they won five to zip."

"Like I said in practice, we'll play possession ball," Coach said. "We'll keep the midfielders back to protect the goal. When you get the ball, play to keep it instead of trying to score."

"Like the Cougars," Elliot said.

"Exactly," Coach said. "We were a better team on paper, but they made it hard for us."

It was a good strategy, but easier said than done. The Bulls offense was always on attack. Fortunately, they missed most of their shots. They made bicycle kicks from forty feet back and tried to shoot the ball through the defenders' legs. Rob couldn't believe it—he'd never seen a team play so over the top like this. After missing a shot, one Bulls player doubled up with laughter while another player patted him on the back.

At halftime the Flyers were only down by two goals. It could have been a lot worse.

"These guys are showing off," Alex grumbled as the team gathered in the locker room.

"Lucky they are or we'd be behind by *ten* goals," Ben said.

"They're not taking us seriously," Rob added. "They think they can toy with us."

"It's their mistake," Coach Tom said. "We're still in this thing."

"I don't know," said Deondre. "I'm beat." Several of the other Flyers agreed, especially the defense.

"And if they have to, they'll get serious," Alex said.

"We can do this," Rob said. "They're just goofing around, and I hate to let 'em win that way."

"Yeah," Ben said. "I don't mind losing to a better team, but to be treated like the game is a joke . . . that bugs me."

The Flyers took the ball deep into Bulls territory at the beginning of the second half. They ran a decoy play. Rob passed to Ben, who flew in front of a defender just in time to avoid being called offside. The Bulls defense swarmed around Rob, expecting him to get the ball again, but Ben passed it to Elliot at midfield and sprinted for the goal. The Bulls defense didn't know who to cover and had to go to man-to-man defense—every defender covered one offensive player.

That always worked in Rob's favor. He could beat anyone one on one. He broke free and Elliot sent a high, arcing kick his way. Rob leaped and headed the ball toward the goal. The goalie leaped and touched the ball, but it skipped off his hand into the net. The Flyers fans went wild.

It wasn't a planned play. Just three guys playing wild, loose soccer. That was Rob's favorite way to play. His love for the game came back to him, coursing through his veins.

The three of them threw their hands into the air and celebrated together.

The Flyers offense gave it everything they had for the rest of the game. Sustaining the attack, watching for mistakes, taking their shots.

The Bulls didn't control the ball as much and didn't waste their chances on wild shots. They did get another goal, but they earned it. They set it up carefully and didn't try anything showy.

They respect us now, Rob thought as he walked off the field. *They didn't show off in the second half.*

"You were outstanding," Coach Tom told him on his way into the locker room.

"Thanks."

"It doesn't seem fair to lose after the way you played."

"That's the way it is," said Rob.

When he checked his phone in the locker room, he saw Tyler had sent him a text: *Want to jam on Saturday?*

Rob sat on a bench and typed out: *I can't. Soccer. Rodgers home game.*

Aw man, really?

He stared at his phone for a solid minute, unsure of how he wanted to respond. He decided to shower instead to clear his head, and he still didn't know what he wanted to say back to Tyler by the time he'd dressed and walked outside.

He was surprised to see his dad waiting for him in the parking lot. "Great game," he said with a toothy grin.

"Oh. Hi. You saw it?"

"I let my assistant take the team through practice today. You were incredible, kiddo."

"Thanks."

"Rob," his dad said, "if you still have any doubts about whether you're a guy who plays soccer as a hobby or a guy with a future in this game . . . Well, you showed me you're for real."

Rob nodded. *I felt that way while I was playing*, he admitted to himself.

"I'm not saying that as your father," his dad said. "I'm saying that as a college coach who would love to sign a kid like you."

He patted Rob on the shoulder. "Come on, we can grab a burger on the way home."

"Really?" Usually his dad wanted to make sure he was eating healthy.

"Why not?" His dad's phone buzzed. He took it out, glanced at it, and frowned before he put it back in his pocket. "Guess I have to drop you off at home after all. Sorry. Take a rain check?"

"Sure."

As Rob trailed behind his dad, he saw a kid in a Harrison High jersey watching them, his mouth hanging open, clearly having recognized his dad. Rob grinned and nodded at him.

I forget that being the soccer star's son can be pretty cool sometimes, he thought. Then he looked at his dad's back in front of him. Rob thought back to Tyler's message, remembering the way he'd felt after scoring the goal earlier today. He thought about what his dad had just said.

Sorry, man. Wish I could.

But he had to focus on soccer. Because the whole team was counting on him. Because he had a soccer career to think about. Because he was for real.

***

The Rodgers soccer team was better than the last time Rob had seen them. Now the players passed to one another on the move without missing a step. They set up plays without having to wave or shout to another player. They were on the same page.

"Told you they'd get there," his dad said after Rodgers scored the first goal of the game.

"I never doubted it," Rob said.

"They're great guys. I don't know if I can . . ." He started to say something, then stopped. "I couldn't ask for a better team," he said instead.

You don't know if you can what? Rob wondered.

Late in the game Rob got a text from Tyler. *Over here.*

He swiveled his head. A hand was waving from the far end of the bleachers.

"Tyler's here," he told his dad, who made a shooing gesture that it was OK to go. Rob walked along the bleachers to the far end where Tyler was standing with Angela and Liz. There was no place to sit because Rodgers students packed the small stadium.

"What are you doing here?" Rob shouted.

"We're here to see you!" Angela playfully poked him in the chest.

"You can get in free after the half," Tyler shouted back. "So we figured we'd walk over."

"Let's go to the concessions," Rob called. It would be quieter over there. He led the way past the bleachers.

He stopped at an open space between two stands and they stood in a circle. "Did you come to watch the last ten minutes of a soccer game?"

"No, we came to ask you if you would play with us," said Liz. Rob felt his stomach flip at that—even though he was ready to focus on soccer again, he realized he was pleased to know they wanted him to play with them again.

From the stands they heard a loud collective groan. The other team must have tied the game. Rob glanced over his shoulder before quickly turning back to the others.

"I don't have my guitar," he said.

"Not tonight," Tyler said. He pulled something up on his phone and handed it to Rob. "In two weeks."

Rob looked at the screen. It was open to a web page:

BATTLE OF THE BANDS
SATURDAY, OCTOBER 6 –
DOORS OPEN AT 4:00 P.M.
ALL BANDS MUST REGISTER BY
SEPTEMBER 21

Rob stopped reading and handed the phone to Tyler. "It's too late to register," he said. "The deadline was yesterday."

"I *did* register us," Tyler told him. "That's why we need you!"

Rob felt his jaw drop in surprise. "You registered me before you asked?"

"I registered the band," Tyler explained. "I thought we could do it as a trio, but we've been playing all night and we sound pretty pathetic without a guitar. Come on, Rob. It'll be fun."

"We're not good enough," Rob argued.

"We only have to play for ten minutes," Angela said. "That's two or three songs. We can get two or three songs down."

Rob paused. *She's right*, he thought. *We already have one song down, and another one we just need to practice a few more times. It really wouldn't take a lot of extra work . . .*

"And we don't expect to win," Liz added. "We just want to be there, to be seen and heard."

"And not sound terrible!" Tyler added.

"But I have soccer," Rob said.

"Not on Saturday night," Tyler said.

"We have a tournament that weekend." *But the game would be done by four o'clock. Sooner if we lose.*

"Two or three good practices," said Tyler. "One gig. That's all we want."

"We'll keep looking for another guitar player, long term," Angela added, "but the Battle of the Bands is in two weeks. We don't have time."

"I guess we could practice Tuesday," Rob said. "And probably next Saturday because my dad has an away game."

"Works for me," Tyler said.

"See if you can get us on late," Rob continued. "I might not be done until later afternoon, then I'll have to shower and run over . . ."

The crowd was standing and slow-clapping now, hoping for a last-second miracle.

"I'll come get you," Liz promised.

"I can't believe you're gonna do it!" Angela surprised him by grabbing his hand and squeezing it. "This is awesome."

The crowd burst into a loud cheer that didn't seem like it would ever end.

"I think Rodgers just scored," said Tyler.

"Yep," said Rob. He glanced toward the steps. "So who wants to go tell my dad about the band?"

ROB explained everything to his dad on the drive home after the game. His dad listened, drawing quick breaths but not arguing or interrupting. Rob was expecting to get a flat-out no.

But his dad surprised him.

"Maybe you need to get this guitar thing out of your system," he said.

"Really? You mean I can do it?"

"Rob, it's your life," his dad said.

Rob nodded. He should have been thrilled, but for some reason he wasn't. Something still felt off. His dad wasn't smiling and saying "Have fun, buddy!" He was all serious, even a little glum.

It's like he's saying, go ahead and make a bad decision, Rob thought.

"But you need to know that your dreams can get away from you," his dad continued. "I had one shot at a World Cup. I wanted to see the US go far, show that we could compete on the world stage. And I wanted America to love soccer the way the rest of the world does. But it didn't happen. We blew it."

Rob knew. The US had been eliminated in the early rounds. Rob was a baby at the time, but he'd heard about it many times. It was clearly one of his dad's biggest regrets in life.

"I thought I would go back there four years later," his dad said. "But you were a toddler and needed me around, so I stopped playing and moved into coaching. I don't have any regrets about that, mind you."

His dad paused, thinking. "My point is that you think you can put that dream on the shelf for a year or two and it'll be there when you come back for it. But then it's gone."

Rob had a feeling his dad wanted him to drop out of the Battle of the Bands but he wanted it to be Rob's idea.

But I'm not going to drop out, he decided. *At least I don't think so.*

***

Rob continued to worry about the decision for the rest of the weekend. He was knotted up inside.

It's one gig and one soccer tournament, he told himself during soccer practice Monday. *This shouldn't be that hard.*

A soccer ball flew by his head.

"Dude, wake up!" said Elliot.

"Sorry!"

The team was standing in groups of three and four, juggling the ball around the circle. The goal was to keep the ball in the air without using their hands. Rob chased down the ball and popped it up with his toe, got it to his knee, and popped it higher. He headed it to Ben. Then he hurried back as Ben volleyed it over to Elliot.

Next they ran a drill called Last Man. One guy had to be the last defender between the other team and the goal. The other players took turns trying to get the ball past him. If one failed, he became the "last man." It was like being *it* in a game of tag.

The last man right now was Ben. He wasn't used to playing defense. Seven guys in a row got past him. He looked tired and irritated.

It was Rob's turn. He dribbled the ball slowly toward Ben, watching him carefully. But suddenly he found himself thinking about the Battle of the Bands.

Did they pick the songs already? Because I like that one about moonlight . . . I forget the name. Angela sure sings it well . . .

Ben stole the ball. He laughed as he kicked it away. "Have fun as last man, Rob."

Rob groaned and took Ben's spot.

Coach Tom caught him on the sideline after practice. "You're off your game today."

"Sorry."

"Everything OK? You aren't hiding an injury, are you?"

"Nope." Rob shook his head. "I just have a lot on my mind."

"Hope you can get your head on straight before Thursday," Coach Tom said.

"Will do."

"It'll make the difference between the A bracket and the B bracket," he said.

"I know." The coach was talking about the tournament. The teams with the best records played in the A bracket, the rest played in the B bracket. *There's no glory in winning the B bracket.*

"We'll be in the A bracket," said Rob. "And we'll win."

***

The knot in his stomach finally untied itself when the band got together on Tuesday. They played through all three songs, and Rob was surprised at how good they sounded. In sync, no muffed chords or missed beats. Music had always helped Rob calm down—apparently even if he was preparing to play in front of a bunch of people.

"We need to tighten up the bridge on that last one to get it under ten minutes," said Liz. "Rob, can you keep your solo to about one bar?"

"Not much of a solo, but sure."

"You can play the full solo when we come out for an encore," she said, adding a *ba-dum-tshh* to show she was kidding. Only the winner would play again, and nobody in the group expected to win.

Rob liked that. *We can enjoy it without having to beat everyone else.*

***

When Rob got home he was surprised to find his father had made dinner. He almost never had time to cook during soccer season. *What's going on?* Rob wondered.

He found out while they ate.

"So, I'm going to go out of town for a couple of days," his dad said. "Leaving tomorrow and back on Friday. You think you'll be OK?"

"Sure."

"It was a last-minute invitation, and I didn't have time to line up someone to stay with you. You seem old for that anyhow."

"I am," Rob said after another bite.

"But you've never been on your own overnight before, so I wanted to make sure."

"Where are you going?"

"LA."

"Really? Why?"

"Business," his dad said.

What kind of business suddenly sends a college soccer coach to LA without a warning? Rob wondered.

Instead of asking, he took another bite and said, "Hey, this is actually good."

His dad grinned, looking relieved that Rob had changed the subject.

After dinner, they washed the dishes together and actually managed to talk about something besides soccer. It was a good evening, but Rob went to bed still not knowing why his dad was going to California for two days.

***

Thursday's game was at home against the Rendell Rhinos. The Rhinos had not won a single game.

"But don't let their record make you cocky," Coach said. "This team is hungry."

"Why don't we buy them some doughnuts?" Elliot asked.

"They must like them. They put enough on the scoreboard," Ben added, elbowing Elliot jokingly. Some of the other players chuckled.

"This is what I'm talking about," Coach said. "You walk out there like it's a cakewalk, you might find yourselves with the doughnut."

"Shouldn't we find ourselves with a cake?" someone joked. The team laughed while Coach Tom shook his head.

It had rained the night before and the field was soggy. That slowed down their game and threw off their timing. The Rhinos didn't fare any better.

"Do you know why you haven't scored?" Coach asked at halftime.

"Because the ground is soggy," said Ben. "It's like playing on a sponge."

"No, because you're playing at their level," Coach said. "You have to pick it up. Especially you, Rob."

"Sorry." *I've been trying*, he thought. But he couldn't deny that he'd been distracted— not just today, but over the past few weeks. Apparently his time with the band had affected his soccer playing more than he'd realized.

"Don't let this one get away from you," Coach said. "You're an A-level team but could land in the B bracket next weekend."

The Flyers nodded at each other and traded fist bumps. Rob began to feel a surge of energy. *All right, all right. Just need to score one goal*, Rob thought. *Put this game away.*

The first time he had the ball in the second half, he tried the give-and-go. He passed it to Ben and sped past the defenders.

Ben sent it back with perfect timing. Rob charged to shoot. His anchor foot slipped on the grass as he kicked, and his kicking foot didn't connect with the ball right. He barely saw the ball fly toward the goal before he fell backward. He wheeled his arms, trying to get his balance, and crashed into one of the other players. His open hand hit the grass, and two of his fingers bent back. Rob expected the pain to come, but he wasn't quite prepared for how much it actually hurt. White-hot pain shot up through his wrist.

Over it all, he heard the crowd cheer.

"THE good news is, you can still play soccer," the doctor told him. Rob was sitting on an exam table, his shoeless feet dangling off the edge. "You want to rest that hand for a few days but no reason to quit for the season." Rob stared at his left hand. Two fingers were fixed with a metal brace and wrapped up with surgical tape. Nothing serious. Just a sprain.

I can play soccer but I can't make a guitar chord, Rob thought. *This is horrible. I wish I'd broken a toe or something instead.* The thought surprised him, but only for a moment. For the first time, Rob realized that if he had to choose, he would rather play the Battle of the Bands than the tournament.

Coach Tom drove him home. He had seen Rob through the entire thing: taken him to the emergency room, called his parents to explain what happened, and waited in the lobby while Rob's finger was set and wrapped.

Rob explained what the doctor had told him, and Coach nodded. "That's great news. But if you need a break, I understand. We'll do the best we can without you."

"Last thing I need is a break on top of this," Rob joked, holding up his injured hand.

"Very funny," Coach Tom said. His voice said it wasn't. They were quiet in the car for a moment.

"Nobody ever gets hurt in an econ class," he said then. "I'm not sure I'm meant to coach."

"You're a good coach," said Rob. "Hey, why did they ask you to coach if you never did it before?"

"Because I've played a lot of soccer. Never at your dad's level. But as far as college."

"What position?"

"Midfielder."

"You good?"

"Sure," Coach Tom said. "My team won the ages-thirty-to-forty park league last year."

"That's something," Rob said with a laugh.

"I'll always play. Even when I'm old and using a cane," said Coach.

"That's cool," said Rob. "And I'm on the opposite end of the spectrum. I'm thinking of quitting," he added suddenly.

"Really?" His coach gave him a glance before looking back at the road. Rob expected him to try to talk him out of it, but Coach just listened.

"I feel like I've put everything into soccer and haven't tried anything else," Rob explained. "Like being in a band. Or trying out for a school play. Or even wasting a weekend playing video games."

"I'm sorry if I've put too much pressure on you," Coach said. "I wanted to be a good coach, so I did what your dad suggested."

"He is a great coach," Rob said. "Players come from all over to play for him."

"But they want to be pros," Coach said. "You have to decide what you want."

He pulled into Rob's driveway. "Here you are."

"Thanks a lot, Coach. For everything."

"Anytime," Coach said. Rob climbed out of the car, grabbed his bag, and walked up to the empty house.

***

When he came downstairs the next morning he saw his dad's suitcase in the hall. His dad was in the living room, dozing on the couch. He opened his eyes and sat up slowly as Rob came into the room.

"Why did you sleep on the couch?"

"I meant to just sit down a minute. How's your hand?"

Rob held up the injured hand. "Sprained but not broken. When did you get home?"

"An hour ago?" his dad guessed, looking at the time on his phone. "When I found out you were hurt I jumped on the next plane home."

"Did you miss any of your . . . business?"

"It's fine," his dad said. "Do you want to take the day off school? Nurse your injury?"

"Nah, it's not that bad," said Rob. He sat down in the armchair. "It's not my writing hand." *But it's the more important hand for guitar. Now I can't even make a chord, let alone do a solo.*

"Think you can still play in the tournament?" his dad asked.

"Sure, but . . ." He took a deep breath. "Dad, I'm thinking about quitting soccer."

"Because you got hurt?"

"No, that's not why. But it helped me come to the decision. I still love the game, but I realized I want to try other things and not spend every waking minute thinking about soccer."

"Wow," said his dad. He rubbed his face with his hand. "This changes things."

"I know," said Rob. "You spent all that money on clinics and camps. Sorry it was a waste."

"It wasn't," his dad said. "The hard work turned you into the amazing kid you are now."

"Yeah, right," Rob said. *He's taking this really well. What's going on?*

"Seriously. I am really proud of you," his dad said. "Soccer or no soccer."

"Thanks, Dad," said Rob. "I better have breakfast and go catch the bus."

"You're serious about this, huh?" his dad said. "I mean, going to school today. Even with the injury? You're not going to milk it?"

Rob laughed from the kitchen. "Yeah, I better go. I have to tell Tyler and the others their guitar player can't make a chord."

***

Tyler texted him on the way to school. He sent a row of weeping emoji, without a single word. *So he knows*, Rob thought. He sent his own row of sad emoji in response.

He saw Angela the moment he walked into history. She looked at his hand and leaped up from her desk.

"Rob! What happened?"

"Soccer injury—fell on it funny."

"Did it hurt?"

"Oh, yeah," he said honestly. "But not anymore. Not much."

She was quiet for a moment. He knew what she wanted to ask.

"I can't play for at least three or four weeks."

"I'm so sorry. That's terrible."

"I know. It means no Battle of the Bands." He shook his head sadly.

"Oh, I thought you meant you can't play *soccer*," she said.

"Oh, yeah. I can play soccer," he said. "I'll play in the tournament. I don't want to let the rest of the team down. Not that I wanted to let the band down," he added hastily.

"It's not like you planned on hurting your hand," she said. "There will always be other shows."

"That's right." He hadn't thought that far ahead. This didn't have to be his only chance to play with them.

***

When Rob got home from school, his dad surprised him by taking him out for dinner. They wolfed down a cheeseburger each and split a basket of onion rings. They didn't talk much, and his dad was in a strange mood. Trying to be friendly, but still tense. He asked Rob three times if he wanted ketchup for his onion rings.

Rob ordered a chocolate and banana malt when the waitress came by to pick up their plates. He was about to make a joke to his dad about not stealing any of the malt, but then he noticed the way his dad took a deep breath and looked up at him.

"Rob, I have a job offer."

"What? Really?" His dad seemed so happy at Rodgers College. Rob couldn't believe it. "Is that why you went to LA?"

"Yes. I met with a lot of people out there. I've been talking with them over the phone for a while now actually. And even though I missed the last meeting, they called today and offered me the job."

"Who? A bigger college?"

"No. I would be working for the US National Team."

"Whoa." That was the biggest imaginable job in soccer. "Will you be their head coach?"

His dad laughed. "No, I'll be a scout at first, maybe an assistant coach when the qualification rounds begin."

"Dad. That is the coolest thing ever," Rob said.

"It'll mean lots of traveling," his dad said. "Weeks at a time in LA, DC, and sometimes other countries . . ."

The waitress brought him his malt. Rob took a couple of sips, barely tasting it.

"Rob, going back to the World Cup would be a dream come true."

"I know. That would be really cool." *Will I get to go and see all the games?* Rob wondered.

Then he realized he had bigger questions. *What will happen to me? Would I travel with Dad? Be alone at the house for weeks at a time?*

"I originally told them I wanted to hold off on a change until you left for college," his dad continued. "But they need their coaching staff in place ASAP. I could barely talk them into waiting until after the Rodgers season."

"What about me?"

"That's the thing. You'd have to go live with your mother. You like Maine, right?"

"Sure, I guess." He'd spent the last four summers there, at least when he wasn't at camp. It was nice. Camping and hiking and canoeing. And he liked spending time with his mom.

Of course, what Dad is talking about is incredible, he thought after a few slurps of his malt. *And since I'm quitting soccer it doesn't matter that the school in Maine doesn't have a team. But all my friends are here. And the band.*

His head started to hurt—he didn't know if it was from the malt or from this news.

"So are you taking the job?" he asked.

"I don't know. But I do know I'm taking that malt." His dad's hand darted in and took the metal cup before Rob could react. "My reflexes are still pretty good, huh?" he said with a teasing smile.

"Now I know how Uruguay feels," Rob said.

EIGHT days later, Rob sat in the locker room at the sports complex where their tournament was taking place. The Flyers had won their first game and moved on to the final game in the A bracket.

Rob had changed into a fresh uniform. The game wasn't for another forty minutes, so he was alone. He was glad for that. He was afraid he would start tearing up and didn't want to do that in front of the other guys.

It's hard to believe this might be my last soccer game, he thought. Rob was going to live with his mom as soon as the quarter ended in early November. His dad would finish the soccer season at Rodgers, then start his new job.

There might be pickup games or rec leagues in Maine, but no school team. And since he wouldn't play the last two years of high school, it would be hard to play in college. At least not for a competitive team.

His parents had let Rob decide: He could finish high school at Fremont and his dad would turn down the job offer. Or Rob could move to Maine and his dad would take the job. Rob had chosen to move. His dad had already stepped away from the World Cup once for him. He wasn't going to ask him to do that again.

There would be plenty to do in Maine, and he was actually looking forward to trying new things. He could ski in the winter and sail in the summer. And his mom had been pestering him for years to hike her favorite mountain with her. Maybe he'd find a band that needed a guitar player or start his own.

It's going to be great, he decided.

Rob walked out to the bench twenty minutes before game time. The stands were already half-full. Tyler, Angela, and Liz had claimed seats in front.

"Hey, you're here!" He was expecting them after the game. Liz was going to drive them to the Battle of the Bands. They were still going, but as audience members instead of competitors.

"We figured we'd watch the big game," said Tyler.

"Good luck," said Angela with a smile.

"Yeah, break a leg," said Liz.

"Uh, I know that's a show business thing, but we don't really say it in sports," Rob said. He held up his hand, where his finger still had a brace and bandage. "It comes true too often."

***

Their game was against the Harrison High Bulls, the only team that had beaten the Flyers all season.

From the moment the game started, the Flyers defense was put to the test. The Bulls held onto the ball and went on a long attack, keeping the ball in play near their goal.

But there were no long shots or bicycle kicks. They were taking the Flyers seriously.

When the Flyers finally got the ball, Luis fed it to Ben and Rob sprinted past his defender. Ben passed him the ball. He judged it perfectly, so Rob and the ball connected without Rob slowing his pace. The Flyers defense rushed in to guard the net.

Rob faked a shot on goal and instead sent the ball back to Ben. He took his own shot and missed, sending the ball out of bounds.

"Nice try," he told Ben as they trotted back and waited for the throw-in.

"Rob!" a voice shouted. He looked up. His dad was three rows back. He'd come even though it was a game day at Rodgers. Rob waved.

"Great setup!" his dad yelled. And for once, that was all. No advice. No coaching. Just cheering him on, like any parent would. The pressure was off. Now he could relax and enjoy the game, win or lose.

The next time he had the ball, Rob made the pass and cruised downfield. Elliot kicked a high, arcing pass to a gap between defenders. Rob ran into the gap, checked that he was onside, and took his best shot.

ABOUT THE AUTHOR

Israel Keats was born and raised in North Dakota and now lives in Minneapolis. He is fond of dogs and national parks.